D1059047

ISBN 0-86163-079-3

Copyright © 1983 Award Publications Limited

First published 1983
10th impression 1995

Published by Award Publications Limited,
1st Floor, Goodyear House,
52-56 Osnaburgh Street,
London NW1 3NS

Printed in Belgium

THE THREE BEARS

Illustrated by RENE CLOKE

AWARD PUBLICATIONS — LONDON

THE THREE BEARS

In a funny little cottage, built in the trunk of a tree, there lived three bears.
Father Bear, Mother Bear and Baby Bear.

They woke up early one morning and decided to go for a walk before breakfast.

"The porridge is too hot to eat" said Mother Bear, "it will have cooled down by the time we get back."

Now, a little girl named Goldilocks had also awakened early.

"I'll go for a walk in the woods," she said, "I've been told not to go alone but I'm sure it's not dangerous."

She wandered a long way through the trees until she came to the bears' cottage.

"What a funny little house!" said
Goldilocks, "I wonder who lives there?"
She knocked at the door, but as there was
no answer, she peeped inside.

The kitchen table was set ready for breakfast.

Bread and honey, cups and saucers, plates, a milk jug and, best of all, three bowls of steaming porridge: big, middle-size and small.

6

"I'm quite hungry after that long walk," said Goldilocks, "I don't suppose anyone will mind if I have just a sip of porridge," and going up to the table, she tasted the porridge in the largest bowl.

"Oh!" she cried, "too much salt! I can't eat that."

So she tried the middle-sized bowl.

This was very, very sugary and, after a few spoonfuls, Goldilocks decided that, although she was so fond of sugar, this was *too* sweet.

"Perhaps the small bowl will be just right," she said, and it was.

It was so lovely that she finished the whole bowlful.

Then she looked around the kitchen.

There were three chairs, big, middle-sized and small, so Goldilocks tried them all.

First she sat in the big chair but this was so big that she was nearly lost in it.

The middle-sized chair wasn't very comfortable for it was rather stiff and hard.

"I think the little chair looks right for me," decided Goldilocks and she sat down in it with a bump.

It was the right size but Goldilocks was much too heavy, one leg broke off and she tumbled to the floor.

Goldilocks was a very inquisitive little girl and now that she had seen the kitchen, she was curious to know what was upstairs.

There was a long winding staircase, so up she went and soon found herself in a funnily-shaped bedroom.

It looked very cosy with pretty curtains at the window and there were three beds.

14

"Big, middle-sized and small," murmured
Goldilocks, "just the same as everything
downstairs.

What a funny little house! I would love to
know who lives here."

Now, Goldilocks had
woken very early that
morning and she had had a
long walk.

"Oh, dear!" she sighed, "I do feel so tired,
I'll just lie down on this big bed for a few
minutes."

The big bed was comfortable but so soft
that Goldilocks was almost smothered by it.

The middle-sized bed was very different; it was so hard that she couldn't feel comfortable which-ever way she turned.

So she decided to try the little bed.

This was just the right size, not too soft and not too hard and very soon Goldilocks had snuggled down and was fast asleep.

When the three bears came back to the
cottage after their walk, they were surprised
to find the door open.

"Someone has been tasting my porridge!" roared Father Bear.

"And someone has been tasting *my* porridge!" growled Mother Bear.

"Someone has tasted *my* porridge," yelled Baby Bear, " and eaten it all up!"

The three bears looked around the kitchen.

"Someone has been sitting in my chair!" grunted Father Bear.

He could see that the two cushions had been moved.

20

"And someone has been sitting in *my* chair" cried Mother Bear.

Baby Bear was furious.

"Someone has been sitting in my chair," he squealed, "and broken it!"

"We will go upstairs," said Father Bear
and up they went.

"Who's been lying on my bed?" he growled.

"And on *my* bed?" echoed Mother Bear.

"Who's been lying on my bed and is fast asleep!" cried Baby Bear.

Their voices roused Goldilocks and she jumped up in a great fright.

"Catch her!"
roared Father Bear.
But Goldilocks
was too quick for
them and she jumped
out of the window.

The three bears
were too fat to get
through the window
and by the time they
reached the front door,
Goldilocks was out of
sight.

She ran through the wood as fast as she could and was soon back in her own home.

"It was a dear little cottage," she said to herself, "but I don't think I'll go that way again."